LEGO® CITY

SKY POLICE!

FROM THE HIT LEGO CITY ADVENTURES TV SHOW!

Adapted by Meredith Rusu

SCHOLASTIC INC.

ISBN: 978-1-338-62591-2

10 9 8 7 6 5 4 3 2 1   20 21 22 23 24

Printed in the U.S.A.   40
First printing 2020

Book design by Cheung Tai

It's a big day in LEGO City. Chief Wheeler has a major announcement.

"Citizens of LEGO City, I'm stoked to reveal our newest weapon against crime: the Sky Police!"

Overhead, the Sky Police planes zoom through the clouds.

"Check them out!" cries Chief Wheeler. "We've got sweet stealth jets and high-powered helicopters!"

"Chief Wheeler, does a lot of crime happen in the sky?" asks a reporter.

"Not anymore!" says the chief. "Because with legendary pro Sergeant Sam Grizzled and his new teammate, Rooky Partnur, leading the force, the sky has never been so safe!"

Meanwhile, Sergeant Grizzled and Rooky Partnur are high in the air flying on patrol.

"Sir, I'm honored to be your partner," says Rooky. "I can't wait to fight crime in the sky!"

Sergeant Grizzled chuckles. "Sorry to break it to you, kid. But there is no crime in the sky."

He turns on the radio. "Attention, all ground units!" a police dispatcher says. "A priceless painting has been stolen from the museum, a crook has stolen millions from a bank, and a dangerous criminal has escaped during a prison transfer!"

"See?" says Sergeant Grizzled. "The real action is on land. Nothing happens up here. I'm a few days away from retirement, so let's sit back, relax, and enjoy the crime-free skies."

Just then, a jumbo jet passes by carrying passengers. Rooky looks over... and spots a suspicious-looking person in the window!

"Sir! Does that masked man look suspicious to you?" she asks.

"Eh, not really," says Sergeant Grizzled. "The mask makes it hard to tell."

But Rooky thinks they should check it out. She turns on the plane's police siren. "Sky Police! Pull over!"

The pilots are confused. "Pull over? Where am I supposed to pull over?" the copilot asks.

"Pull over by that cloud!" Rooky shouts.

The planes stop in midair, side-by-side. Rooky makes the leap over to the jumbo jet. "I have reason to believe there's a person of interest on your plane," she tells the pilots.

On board, Rooky searches row by row for the masked man. But she isn't watching where she's going, and she slips on a little boy's toy in the aisle.

"Rooky, all okay over there?" Sergeant Grizzled calls over the walkie-talkie.

"I fell down," she replies. But her walkie-talkie has static.

"I do not copy," Sergeant Grizzled says. "There's too much static."

"I fell down!" Rooky repeats loudly.

But all Sergeant Grizzled hears is "I—down!"

"Officer down!" he cries into his police intercom. "All Sky Police units, I need backup—stat!"

Within minutes, the entire Sky Police force is flying to the rescue!

Sergeant Grizzled leaps aboard the jumbo jet. "I thought you were down?" he says.

"No, I tripped and fell down." Rooky explains.

"You mean I just jumped between two planes at twenty thousand feet days before retirement for nothing?" Sergeant Grizzled exclaims.

"Not for nothing," says Rooky. "We still need to find that masked man!"

Together, they search the plane. Suddenly, the jet hits a bumpy patch of air and all the overhead compartments open up. Luggage comes tumbling down . . . including the stolen painting!

"It's the missing painting!" Rooky gasps. "And there's the masked man—he's the thief! And he's on this plane!"

The masked man breaks away and races to the cargo bay. In there, he discovers the bank crook, and the escaped convict. All three bad guys are on board!

"How weird is it that we all have to get off the same plane?" laughs the thief.

"I figured I could escape easier in the sky, because crime never happens up here," says the convict.

"You couldn't make this stuff up!" cackles the bank crook.

But Rooky isn't about to let them get away that easily. She and Grizzled chase them to the top of the plane. "Stop, by order of the Sky Police!" Rooky shouts. "I have handcuffs, and I'm not afraid to use them!"

The Sky Police have the bad guys cornered. But the crooks jump off the plane and open three parachutes! "They're getting away!" moans Rooky.

"Not if I have anything to say about it," says Grizzled. "I was saving these jetpacks for my retirement adventures, but it looks like the call of duty doesn't wait. Let's go!"

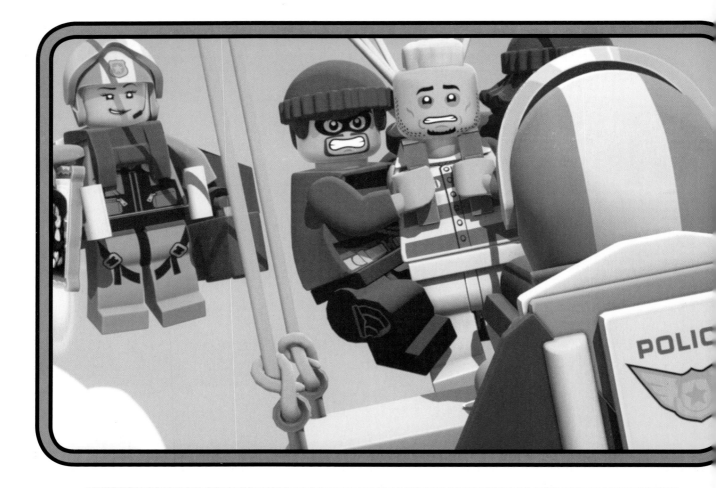

Rooky and Grizzled use the jetpacks to zoom down and corner the three bad guys—in midair!

"Freeze, in the name of the Sky Police!" orders Sergeant Grizzled.

Rooky grins and holds up the handcuffs. "Told you I wasn't afraid to use these."

Back on the ground, the criminals get shipped off to jail. "Great job, Sky Police," their fellow officer Duke Detain says. "This city is lucky to have you."

"Thanks, Duke. But the credit goes to my partner," says Grizzled. "She did everything."

"Aw, thanks, Sergeant," Rooky blushes.

"No, thank you," says Grizzled. "That was a pretty high-flying case to go out on. I guess crime really does happen in the sky."

Rooky grins. "But as long as the Sky Police are on duty, we know the skies will stay safe."